STO

FRIENDS
OF ACPL

P9-EFJ-172

Books by Matt Christopher

Sports Stories

THE LUCKY BASEBALL BAT
BASEBALL PALS
BASKETBALL SPARKPLUG
TWO STRIKES ON JOHNNY
LITTLE LEFTY
TOUCHDOWN FOR TOMMY
LONG STRETCH AT FIRST BASE
BREAK FOR THE BASKET
TALL MAN IN THE PIVOT
CHALLENGE AT SECOND BASE
CRACKERJACK HALFBACK
BASEBALL FLYHAWK
SINK IT, RUSTY
CATCHER WITH A GLASS ARM
WINGMAN ON ICE
TOO HOT TO HANDLE
THE COUNTERFEIT TACKLE
THE RELUCTANT PITCHER

LONG SHOT FOR PAUL
MIRACLE AT THE PLATE
THE TEAM THAT COULDN'T LOSE
THE YEAR MOM WON THE
    PENNANT
THE BASKET COUNTS
HARD DRIVE TO SHORT
CATCH THAT PASS!
SHORTSTOP FROM TOKYO
LUCKY SEVEN
JOHNNY LONG LEGS
LOOK WHO'S PLAYING FIRST BASE
TOUGH TO TACKLE
THE KID WHO ONLY HIT HOMERS
FACE-OFF
MYSTERY COACH
ICE MAGIC

Animal Stories

DESPERATE SEARCH

Desperate Search

Desperate Search

by
Matt Christopher

Illustrated by Leslie Morrill

Little, Brown and Company

BOSTON   TORONTO

COPYRIGHT © 1973 BY MATTHEW F. CHRISTOPHER

ALL RIGHTS RESERVED. NO PART OF THIS BOOK MAY BE REPRODUCED IN ANY FORM OR BY ANY ELECTRONIC OR MECHANICAL MEANS INCLUDING INFORMATION STORAGE AND RETRIEVAL SYSTEMS WITHOUT PERMISSION IN WRITING FROM THE PUBLISHER, EXCEPT BY A REVIEWER WHO MAY QUOTE BRIEF PASSAGES IN A REVIEW.

FIRST EDITION

T 10/73

Library of Congress Cataloging in Publication Data

Christopher, Matthew F
  Desperate search.

  SUMMARY: Trying to help each other get home during a blizzard, two lost pets become closer friends, as do the two boys searching for them.
  [1. Friendship—Fiction] I. Morrill, Leslie, illus. II. Title.
PZ7.C458De   [Fic]   73-7741
ISBN 0-316-139599

Published simultaneously in Canada
by Little, Brown & Company (Canada) Limited
PRINTED IN THE UNITED STATES OF AMERICA

1776907

To Jack, Marianne, Erin and Shannon

Desperate Search

1

It was two days before Christmas in the
sleepy little town of Joberg in upstate New
York.

Whitey, a white Persian cat sitting in the
sun at the corner outside of Bundy's Grocery
Store, stirred. His eyes widened into round,
perfect circles. His long fur bristled.

A boy and a dog were coming down the
road.

Whitey heard the door of the store open and
glanced around, hoping it was the boy with
whom he had come. But it wasn't. It was an
older man who must have gone into the store
earlier. Bundled in a gray winter coat and

carrying a bag of groceries, he smiled at Whitey and shuffled down the snow-caked walk to a car.

Whitey watched him put the groceries in the car, get in, and drive away.

Then he looked back up the road, and the black elongated pupils in his yellow eyes focused sharply on the boy and the dog.

They were still beyond the intersection on the same side of the road that Whitey was on, and they were approaching at a leisurely gait.

The boy was black and about the same size and build as Whitey's master. He was friendly and well-mannered. But Whitey knew that the dog, Ginger, wasn't.

The two animals had met on previous occasions. Ginger always wanted Whitey's attention, and Whitey always tried to ignore her. But not even his firm cat commands could discourage Ginger, who would keep persisting, drawing closer, and barking that harsh bark of hers. She was a fresh, intolerable animal who refused to give up.

4

Whitey waited. The boy and dog paused momentarily at the intersection, watched carefully for cars, then ran across, slowing down as they reached the other side.

Between the store and the intersection was a house with a large front lawn. Ginger was at the edge of the lawn when she suddenly spotted Whitey and stopped. Her long, fluffy tail started to wag and she barked. Then she bolted forward, tail and mouth going at the same time.

"Ginger! No!" the boy yelled.

Ginger ignored him. The boy yelled again, running toward her, but the dog apparently didn't hear or just refused to obey.

Five feet from Whitey Ginger crouched on her belly and looked at the cat with wide, imploring eyes. Her ears were long, her tongue was hanging out, and her brown and white coat was smudged with dirt.

Whitey arched his back, his mustached lips pulling away from his teeth exposing his extra-long, menacing side molars. As he kept an alert, cautious guard, he extended his forepaws in front of him, claws ready for action.

Ginger crept closer, barked, and made a surprising leap forward.

"Meowrrr!" Whitey shrieked and sprang backward, both paws lifted to rake Ginger's black nose should she dare pounce.

Ginger stopped inches away from the bared claws, leaped back, then bolted forward again, barking in a way that did not sound angry, but which disgusted Whitey nevertheless.

Whitey, who lived with the Nooley family, enjoyed a privilege few other felines could boast. Most cats with whom he had come in contact during his brief excursions outdoors were allowed indoors only at night, or else they slept in a basket on a porch and had to resort to mice or bird-hunting to completely satisfy their hunger.

Not so with Whitey. He lived indoors day and night, winter and summer, and his food was served to him in a special dish. Because of his distinguished breed, he was selective about his friends, and, as a result, he had so few he could count them on one paw (were he able to count). As a matter of fact, there were only two whom he actually looked forward to seeing, and both were females. His other acquaintances were males, none of whom he could encounter without getting into a fight.

A natural instinct told him that this overgrown, conceited dog was also a female, but her sex didn't make a bit of difference. A dog was a dog, and dogs had no business in a cat's life.

"Stay here, Ginger," the boy ordered as he went into the store. "I'll be out in a minute."

Whitey looked hopefully at the door, waiting for it to open again and his master to emerge. But it didn't open, and he was left to face Ginger's irritating teasing.

Suddenly a thunderous roar broke the silence, startling both animals. A huge truck lumbered up, its high, black wheels menacing, and stopped in front of the store. For a moment Ginger watched it, her tongue still dangling from her mouth. Then she looked at Whitey. A mischievous gleam sparkled in her brown eyes, and Whitey wondered what she had in mind.

He remained still, hoping that Ginger would go and do her own investigating and not bother him any more. At the same time he remained alert in case she tried a surprise lunge at him.

His ears perked up at the sound of a slamming door. He watched a man's legs step down from the left side of the truck and come around toward the rear. Then the man, a fellow somewhat taller than his own master and a good deal older, came fully into sight as he opened up the truck's rear doors. Stored inside was a vast assortment of boxes.

The man hopped into the back of the truck, pulled down several boxes from the pile, hopped out, and carried two of them into the store.

Whitey watched with avid interest, and it dawned on him that the truck could be his

8

refuge. There was ample space between some of the piles of boxes through which he could squeeze to hide from Ginger, who simply refused to give up pestering him.

Slowly he rose up on his four paws, his eyes never leaving Ginger. Then, in a move that caught her by surprise, he lunged past her, leaped into the truck, and squeezed through the pile of boxes toward the rear where he was sure he would be safe for the time being.

He turned around and lay down, his face comfortably resting on his forepaws. A little while later the man came back for some of the remaining boxes and carried them inside.

Whitey heard Ginger bark just outside the open doors, but he couldn't see her. Then the barking stopped. Whitey waited, his ears perked, straining for the next sound. His large eyes watched the opening with mounting anxiety. His body was as still as a rock. Nothing about him moved except the tip of his tail, which curled one way and then the other and his heart, which kept beating fast.

9

Suddenly a dark streak shot up into the opening, and Whitey bolted up on all fours. His back arched, the fur rising in tufts from his hide. His lips curved back in seething anger, for there stood that obnoxious dog inside the truck, looking at him with a pleased glint in her mischievous eyes, her tongue dangling and pulsing almost as if it had a life of its own.

His heart beating even faster now, Whitey watched, waiting for Ginger's next move. One thing for certain, Whitey wasn't afraid of her. He was just terribly annoyed with her rambunctious child-play and wanted no part of it.

The sound of a latch opening registered in Whitey's ears, and for an instant his ears pricked. At the same time, as if she had heard it too, Ginger looked quickly around, and then she bolted almost soundlessly up a pile of boxes at the cat's right. Only the scraping of her nails against the cartons betrayed her position.

Whitey, who had shrunk back momentarily

at the sudden, unexpected move, now looked up to find Ginger. But she was out of sight now, sitting or lying on a box close to the roof.

Escape and freedom from Ginger now seemed to be in order for Whitey. He stood up and took a step toward the opening at the rear of the truck, only to shrink back again as heavy footsteps crunched the frozen ground. Quickly one door slammed shut and then the other, the sound of inevitable doom. And everything was black.

Whitey heard footsteps crossing around to the side of the truck, the motor starting up, the grinding of a gear, and finally he felt the truck moving. He remained still in the darkness, his heart pounding.

It was tragic enough that he couldn't see, but it was worse that he couldn't do anything.

2

Tommy Nooley was almost ready to leave the store when Jamie Gilman entered.

"Hi, Jamie," Tommy greeted him. "You going to be long?"

"No. Just got to get a few things."

"I'll wait for you," said Tommy.

He and Jamie knew each other, but they were not close friends. Although they lived only a few hundred yards from each other, there always seemed to be an invisible barrier between the two homes. Tommy couldn't explain why it was nor what it was. He just knew it was there.

He placed the large bag of groceries on the

end of the counter and waited for Mr. Bundy, a large-framed man, to get the groceries as Jamie called them off his list.

"Three pounds of tomatoes," Jamie said.

Mr. Bundy, whistling a happy tune through his teeth, lumbered over to the produce section, picked up two handfuls of bright red tomatoes from a bin, and placed them on a scale.

"Three pounds, eh? Let's see . . . that's two and a quarter. A coupla more should do it. There. Exactly three pounds on the button. What else, Jamie?"

"Mom wants me to pick up that turkey," Jamie said.

"Oh. The one she ordered last week. Yes, sir. One turkey coming up. Got your tree up already, Jamie?" he asked as he headed toward the freezer at the back of the store.

"Had it up since day before yesterday," Jamie said.

"Good. Hoping for something special for Christmas, or are you going to be satisfied with whatever you get?" Mr. Bundy chuckled and went on talking before Jamie had a chance to answer. "Ever have an electric train set? I mean a HO set, the small kind that runs on those tiny tracks?"

"No," Jamie said.

Tommy caught Jamie's eyes and shrugged. If Mr. Bundy's hundred-year-old cash register were to open and close in one day as often as his mouth did, he'd be a millionaire.

Mr. Bundy returned with a frozen turkey, still gabbing about the HO train set, when the door opened and a short, stocky man entered carrying a couple of wooden boxes.

"Hi, Jake!" said the man. "Here comes Santa Claus bringing you gifts of joy! Ho! Ho! Ho!"

" 'Scuse me, Jamie," Mr. Bundy said, "while I show Santa Claus where to put that stuff. You're in no hurry, are you?"

Jamie shrugged. "No."

"I'll be back in a shake of a tail," Mr. Bundy said. Then he turned to the delivery man. "I'll have to fix you a spot for them supplies in the

14

back room, Mike. Forgot you were coming a day earlier this week."

"It'll be the same next week, Jake. Good thing Christmas and New Year's come only once a year."

"Quit complaining," Mr. Bundy said. "If you were inside all day like I am you'd have corns on top of corns and callouses on top of callouses."

They chattered back and forth all the time they were in the back room. Then the delivery man walked out of the store and returned a few moments later with more boxes. Finally, both men went up to the counter, where the delivery man gave Mr. Bundy an order slip, and Mr. Bundy paid him.

"Looked at that western sky lately?" the delivery man asked. "It's getting blacker than Hades. And this time of the year it ain't rain, man. It's a blizzard."

"Let 'er come," Mr. Bundy said, as he took the order slip and turned to the cash register. "I'm not going anywhere, anyway."

He pushed a lever, and the cash box flew out with a bang. He took out some bills and change and handed them to the man.

"Here you are, Mike," he said. "And a little extra for yourself. Have a Merry Christmas."

"Thanks, Jake. And you, too. So long. See you next week."

The door clattered shut behind him as he walked out.

"Sorry to hold you up, Jamie," Mr. Bundy apologized. "But I'd forgot that Smalls would be delivering today. Let's see, now. You got your turkey. Anything else?"

"Two dozen rolls and a pound of cheese, and that'll be it," Jamie said.

Mr. Bundy got the things for him, put the turkey into one bag and the other groceries into another, then figured up the items on the cash register.

"Nine hundred and twenty-two pennies," he said, pushing a button that made the cash box fly open again.

Jamie handed him a ten-dollar bill. "That's all I've got," he said, smiling.

Mr. Bundy took it, looked it over, and smiled. "Looks good to me," he said. He put it in a tray and counted out seventy-eight cents in change onto Jamie's palm.

"Have a nice Christmas, Jamie," he said. "And say hello to your Mom and Dad for me."

"I will. And the same to you, Mr. Bundy."

"Merry Christmas to you, too, Tommy."

"Same to you, Mr. Bundy," Tommy said, and he and Jamie walked out into the cool sunshine.

"Man!" Tommy exclaimed. "He can talk a guy's head off!"

The two boys started to walk up the road. Then they both stopped at the same time, looked behind them, and then all around.

"Ginger!" Jamie yelled.

"Whitey!" Tommy shouted.

They paused and then looked at each other with expressions of great concern coming over their faces.

"Whitey!" Tommy called again. "Here, Whitey! Whitey!"

"Ginger! Come here, girl! Come here, Ginger!"

Nothing.

Tommy's eyes hardened as he looked again at Jamie. "Ginger probably chased after him. She does every time she sees Whitey."

"She just wants to play," Jamie said.

"But Whitey doesn't. He doesn't like her."

"I know," Jamie said. "But I'm sure Ginger likes Whitey. She always goes to Whitey because she wants to make friends."

"Then where are they now?" Tommy asked, trying hard to hold back his anger. "Why aren't they here now?"

"I don't know," Jamie said.

They looked up and down the road. From where they stood they could see almost every house in the north side of Joberg.

Tommy's eyes lifted upward to the sky where massive gray clouds floated by like huge armies on the march. The remark the Smalls delivery man had made about the possibility of a blizzard looked more and more likely to come true.

18

"Tommy, look," Jamie said suddenly.

Tommy turned and saw Jamie pointing at paw prints in the hard-packed snow.

"They're Ginger's!" Jamie said excitedly. "I bet a dollar they are! She was standing here! No — it looks like she jumped! The prints are deeper in this spot than they are back there!"

"Jumped?" Tommy frowned. He began to think hard, turning over the possibilities in his mind, until he came up with a solution that made sense. He looked at the deep prints made by the truck's tires a few feet ahead of the paw prints, and thought: *if Ginger was jumping that could mean she'd been trying to get into the truck. But why?*

"Jamie," he said, "do you think Ginger would try to get into the truck after something to eat?"

"I've tried to teach her better manners than that," Jamie answered. "But that's what she did. She jumped into the truck."

"You sure?"

"I'm sure, all right. Those tracks prove it."

20

"You know what I think?" said Tommy. "I think that Whitey jumped up into the truck to get away from Ginger and that Ginger followed him. Both must have still been in the truck when the delivery man closed the door."

Jamie's eyes widened. "I bet you're right, Tommy."

"Jamie, we have to go after that truck!"

"*Run* after it?" Jamie stared at Tommy as if Tommy had gone out of his mind.

"No. We'll take the groceries home and I'll get Buck. You want to run in the store and ask Mr. Bundy where that truck is stopping next?"

Jamie ran in and a minute later was back again. "He doesn't know," Jamie said. "All he knows is that Mike what's-his-name goes to Danning. There's a store between here and Danning, but Mr. Bundy doesn't know if the guy'll stop there or not."

"C'mon. Let's hurry home," said Tommy.

The walk was a half a mile, and after the halfway point, it became more and more tedi-

21

ous each step of the way. But imagining the dangers the animals might encounter kept both boys going.

Jamie suggested that one of them telephone the store Mr. Bundy had said was halfway between Joberg and Danning.

"I'll ask my mother to do it," said Tommy.

He asked her the moment he entered the house. She was familiar with the store, she said, and she knew who owned it — a Mr. Manley. She telephoned immediately, only to learn that the truck had left less than two minutes ago.

"I'm going to get Buck, Mom," Tommy said, his nerves strung as tightly as banjo strings. "Jamie's going with me."

"But, Tommy! You really don't know where that truck is going!"

"Mr. Bundy said it's going to Danning."

"That's fifteen miles from here!"

"Buck can do it, Mom. We've traveled more miles than that lots of times."

He started for the door, but his mother

stopped him. She was small, oval-faced, and blue-eyed, with a capacity for keeping on the go every minute of the day. She seemed to think that the world would end if she stopped a minute to rest. Yet Tommy remembered the days when he was sick and she had stayed beside him, consoling and comforting him. It seemed that during moments of need she was always there. Dad was as loving as she, but because he was away at work most of the time, it was Mom whose presence and warmth he felt constantly.

"There's a storm coming, Tommy," she warned him. "It might hit us within the next hour."

"We'll be careful."

She touched his face. Her hand was smooth, tender. She inhaled deeply, and sighed. "I know how much Whitey means to you. And how much Ginger means to Jamie. I was a little girl once, and I know."

He looked at her imploringly. "Can I go now, Mom?"

"All right," she said. "But get to a phone . . . if you need help."

"Okay, Mom. Bye."

He ran to the small barn across the creek, saddled up the fudge-colored, three-year-old quarter horse, Buck, and rode up the road to Jamie's house, wondering if Jamie's mother would let him go looking for Ginger. His heart leapt with joy as he saw Jamie waiting for him on the porch. The boy raced to the road, wearing a scarf around his neck. Tommy helped him climb up behind him.

He jabbed his heels into Buck's ribs, and the horse leapt forward, his butterscotch mane flying in the wind, his hooves rhythmically clopping the snow-packed road. Tommy had gotten Buck a year ago last summer, answering an advertisement in the *Money Saver,* a paper distributed to the residents in the township. He had wanted a horse ever since he was seven years old, but his parents thought he should wait until he was older.

Buck had been two years old when Tommy

and his father bought him, and it was no time at all before Tommy and Buck were close friends. Tommy rode him with no fear whatever. His parents owned ten acres of land, which his father tilled and grew crops on every year to help supplement his income. All of the land stretched out in glorious rolling fields behind their home, and Tommy and Buck played and romped on it for hours. Often Whitey perched behind Tommy in the saddle. At first the cat had been timid, but by now the riding had become almost second nature to him.

"Think we'll ever catch up with that truck, Tommy?" Jamie asked.

"We're not going to stop until we do catch up with it, Jamie," Tommy promised.

As they rode on, Tommy wondered how long Buck could run before he became winded and needed to slow down. Buck was in fine condition, but he wasn't a machine. He could not be expected to run continuously for an hour or so without a break. Playing hard and romping in the fields was different. Then he could rest when he felt like it. Now he had to go on without breaks.

Tommy looked at the sky in the northwest. It was gray black, a foreboding sign.

"How long do you think it'll be before that storm hits us, Jamie?" he asked, a faint tremor in his voice.

"Three-quarters of an hour. Maybe an hour. It doesn't look good, Tommy."

3

Whitey lay in the truck, his eyes wide open, staring into the darkness that had enveloped him ever since the rear doors of the truck had closed.

Much of the fright that had initially gripped him had worn off. Now he felt puzzled and uneasy. The sense of movement, the frequent, gentle bumps, and the steady hum of a powerful motor told him that he was being carried swiftly over a road.

He thought of Tommy, and his heart beat faster. Tommy was Whitey's dearest friend. Not even another cat could be as dear to him as Tommy was. The two were almost always together. Now his separation from Tommy left a pang in Whitey's heart.

He remembered Ginger sitting on top of one of the boxes above him, and his head tipped backward while his eyes strained to penetrate the darkness. But they couldn't, so he lowered his head again and relaxed, comforted by the thought that, for a while at least, he wouldn't be pestered by the frisky, young dog.

Suddenly he was lifted and dropped with some force as the truck struck a pothole in the road, and an involuntary mew broke from his lips.

Almost at the same time he heard a soft whimper above him. He looked up, but he relaxed again when there was no further sound.

The truck continued on its rough, bumpy way, the sound of the motor suggesting that it was traveling at a fast rate of speed. At one point it slowed down, the horn blatting loudly, and then it picked up speed again.

Dejected, helpless — at least for the time

being — Whitey laid his head down on his forepaws and closed his eyes. There was nothing to do now but wait. Somewhere along the road the truck would have to stop again.

A new sound in the hum of the motor suggested to him that the time was about to come. He opened his eyes, perked up his ears, and listened.

The truck slowed down, rolled over a shallow bump, and stopped. The motor died. A door squeaked open, slammed shut. A musical whistle started up outside and seemed to be headed toward the rear of the truck. Then a bell clanged as another door opened and closed, shutting out the sound of the whistle.

The cat waited, his fur stiff on his hide, his ears alert. The dark world surrounding him was silent. A sense of fear began to take hold of him. He cried out softly, "Meow!" paused a few moments, then cried out again, "Meow!"

Oh, if only Tommy was within earshot of his voice. He would hear. He would help.

The thought of Tommy made the cat de-

29

spair. He longed for his human friend to rescue him from this dark adventure into the unknown. He mewed for his friend's presence and companionship.

Unable to lie still, he rose and edged through the pile of unseeable boxes. Their rubbing against him was a comforting feeling, though nothing was quite like the warm and tender stroke of the boy's gentle hand.

He heard the bell clang again, and guided by the boxes, he turned and hurried back to the front of the truck. When his head bumped the wall he turned around and stood facing the opposite direction, waiting for the doors to open. He heard, instead, the grinding sound of the driver's door opening. Then he felt the truck tilt as the man stepped into the cab, and he knew that the doors would not open for him, that he would remain a prisoner here indefinitely.

As the motor started up and the truck lurched forward, Whitey curled up and lay down. Once again he heard the gears mesh as the truck picked up speed. Then the motor settled into an even hum, and he felt himself whisked over the rough, bumpy road.

Sometime later the truck stopped again. Surprisingly the rear doors opened, and from his hiding place Whitey stared in fear as the delivery man lifted out several boxes and carried them into a store. First one ear twitched and then the other as the cat thought over the prospect of escaping. But the place was strange. The fear of coping with the unknown outside made him hesitate.

He rose on his forepaws, his pupils dilated as he looked out at the bleak but welcome daylight. He blinked tiredly, swished his tail from side to side, then held still as he heard a door somewhere open and close.

The man came back, whistling the tune he had whistled before, and closed the truck doors, shutting Whitey and Ginger up again in their black prison.

Again the tilt of the truck, the grinding sound of the starter, the hum of the motor, the

31

lurch forward, the ride over the road. But now the ride was smooth, comfortable. Only the whirring sound of the tires, mixed with the hum of the motor, gave Whitey the feeling that he was being carried away swiftly to some unknown destination.

He rested his chin on his paws and closed his eyes, thinking of the boy, the dog, and the good life he had left behind.

He slept.

Sometime later he awakened suddenly, his ears straightening, his eyes staring into the darkness. The sensation of movement was gone. The sound of the motor had died. There was no sound at all, nothing that reached his acute sense of hearing.

He became frightened, and his fur rose stiffly on his hide. Then he heard a faint, distant hum varying in sound, but he recognized it as only the wind. For a long time he sat there, staring straight ahead in the direction where he remembered the doors to be, hoping they would open.

He remained in that position a long time, waiting for a new sound. And, at last, it came.

But it came from inside the truck, from the dog lying quietly above him on one of the boxes. It was a soft, intermittent whine, as if she were getting restless.

The whine continued for a while longer, and during that time a gradual change came over Whitey. As disgusted and angry as he was before at Ginger, he was feeling pleased and comforted now. Something about Ginger's cry suggested a feeling that was close to his own — a feeling of fear, no doubt growing all the while they both had been riding in this intense darkness — and a desire to have this mysterious ride come to an end.

Whitey rose, a real warmth in his heart, and purred as he stretched his legs and arched his back to relieve his stiff, cramped body. He strode between the boxes to the back of the truck, then back and forth along the side of the doors, his eyes intent on the stringlike crack of daylight he was able to see between the bottom of the doors and the floor of the truck.

Suddenly he heard a door in the distance open and ease shut. Familiar footsteps approached the back of the truck. A familiar whistling sound emitted from a man's lips.

Whitey's peaked ears twitched as he bent his head down close to the crack between the door and floor, and he waited.

1776907

4

Tommy and Jamie rode around the bend, past farms, fields of skeletal cornstalks, mobile homes, and a stretch of woods on both sides of the road. At last, far ahead, they saw the red sign that told them they were nearing Manley's Store.

There was no reason to stop, though. They knew that the truck had already been there and that nothing had been delivered. Therefore, if the doors hadn't been opened, the animals must still be inside.

They rode past the store, and on and on, Buck's pounding hooves a rhythmic, drumlike sound in the boys' ears.

"How far's Danning from Joberg, Tommy?" Jamie shouted over the wind.

"Fifteen miles, exactly!" Tommy answered.

"How many miles do you think we've gone so far?"

"Maybe ten . . . eleven!"

The storm clouds were approaching from the northwest, coming from across Lake Kelsey. Minutes later the first flakes of snow began swirling through the sky, showering the boys' faces.

"The blizzard's here, Tommy!" Jamie cried.

"Yeah! Well, we're not going to turn back now! Unless you want to stop at Danning and call up your folks to come and get you!"

"No! I won't do that!" Jamie said. "Maybe we'll find Ginger and Whitey there!"

"Maybe!"

The wind seemed to double in strength within the next few minutes. Now and then a violent gust forced the horse away from the side of the road. Tommy pulled the collar of his coat up as high as he could around his face, and Jamie wrapped the scarf around his.

The snow was coming down thick and hard now, melting on their faces till it looked like tears running down their cheeks. It was clinging to the ground and covering up the dirty patches of old, packed-down snow. A car crawled by, the driver staring out at the three, amazement and worry clouding his eyes.

"He probably thinks we're nuts riding in this weather!" Jamie cried.

"Maybe we are!" Tommy yelled over his shoulder.

"Yeah!" said Jamie, laughing. The laughter, carried through the wind to Tommy, was contagious and Tommy laughed, too.

Though the search was an anxious one for the two boys, riding Buck took the edge off the worry. Even though the truck led them by several miles and was constantly gaining, riding the horse was still hundreds of times better than walking. But Tommy knew that even if he had had to walk after Whitey, he would have. And probably Jamie would have done the same for Ginger, too.

Jamie. Tommy thought about him a minute. This was the first time they had been together for any length of time. It seemed to Tommy that the only other times they had seen each other were on the bus going to and from school. Or when they happened to meet each other going to Mr. Bundy's store.

They rode on past homes that looked silent and deserted, the snow whirling around them like moths flitting around a flower before lighting. Tommy cried out as he recognized the square brick structure of their school ahead of them. As they rode by he smiled at the cutout figures pasted on the windows, remembering that members of his own class had had to do the same thing before school had closed for the Christmas vacation. The violent flapping of the cords against the flagpole was like a gauge measuring the angry gusts of the wind.

Finally they plodded into the town of Danning. Just before the intersection they pulled off to the right at a large supermarket, and Tommy drew Buck to a halt.

"Go in, Jamie," he said, "and ask if that Smalls truck has stopped here yet."

Jamie slid off the horse and ran into the store. A bell clanged as he opened the door, and clanged again as it closed behind him. As Tommy waited, he watched the snow pelting Buck on the side of his face, building up into a white blanket on his mane and melting on his warm hide. Already about an inch had fallen, coming down in thick flakes now, swirling, spiraling, landing to join with the others.

A few minutes later the doorbell clanged again, and Jamie came running out.

"Said he didn't see a cat or dog!" he yelled.

Tommy pulled him up behind him. "He said that even if either one was out here he wouldn't have seen them," Jamie continued breathlessly, "because he hasn't been outside since he opened up the store at seven o'clock this morning!"

"That's about what I thought," reflected Tommy. "Did you ask him which way the truck went after it left here?"

"That way." Jamie pointed to the road leading to the left at the intersection.

Tommy held Buck back till a car passed by, then prodded him in the ribs with the heels of his shoes. "Did you ask him how long ago the truck left?"

"I didn't think about that," said Jamie. "Shall I ask him?"

"Not now! Every second we stop is wasted time!"

He was suddenly angry, angry at Jamie and himself for not thinking about it sooner.

Buck plodded diagonally across the intersection, then began to sprint, fresh again after the short rest. Tommy knew that the road took them in the direction of Lake Kelsey and that some three or four miles farther on it would wind to the right till it ran parallel with the lake. What was the next town beyond that? Carl Point? And how far away was it? Seven or eight miles?

The prospect of continuing on to Carl Point was frightening. By the time they reached it the snow would be a foot deep. Tommy noticed that the wind had slackened, but now the snow was falling in thicker flakes, like soft feathers from a million open pillows.

On the right they passed by a church and a rectory. Behind them a cemetery lay in profound silence, the snow piling up on the monuments like white headdresses. Soon Danning was behind them.

Tommy wondered what time it was. He had no watch, but he surmised that daylight would last another hour. With this heavy snowfall there wouldn't be a twilight. Night would fall like a black curtain. What would they do then? Should they go on? To where? They knew neither the final destination of the truck, nor even where it came from originally.

Common sense urged Tommy to go back. His conscience confirmed that returning home now was the smart thing to do before the snow got much deeper and all three of them were caught in real trouble.

But his heart ached as he thought of Whitey,

ached as he visualized him cooped up inside the truck, probably freezing. Whitey had been stricken with bronchitis once, and two or three times after that had suffered from colds which had required the attention of a veterinarian. Unless he were rescued from the imprisonment of the truck, he might be stricken again, and pneumonia could develop. He could die.

No, Tommy thought despairingly, *I can't go back now. I have to keep on going. Somewhere ahead are Whitey and Ginger. Jamie and I will find them. We have to.*

5

The doors of the truck opened. Whitey stood inside, the brightness of daylight blinding him for a moment. Only a few feet away with snow falling on him was the delivery man, staring wide-eyed in astonishment.

"Hey!" the man shouted. "How'd you get in there? *When* did you get in there?"

A dog's bark ripped the air. There was a thumping of paws, a grating of claws on boxes, and the man stared at the dog that had bounded down beside the cat.

"Hey!" the man cried. "Haven't I seen you before?"

Even as the man said this, Whitey sensed that the time to depart from this undesirable situation had come.

He jumped, landing soundlessly on his padded paws in the feather-light snow, and ran underneath the truck toward a building close by. He heard a bark behind him and glanced back just long enough to see that Ginger was following him.

Strange, but Whitey wasn't anxious to get away from the dog now. On the contrary, he was *glad* to hear that bark which not too long ago had annoyed him terribly. He was *glad* to know that Ginger was close behind him.

Whitey had no idea where he was. Nothing about the building, the trees, or the field beyond looked familiar at all. He reached the opposite side of the building, paused and looked back. He saw Ginger stop, too, still and tall in the snow, her eyes held sharply on his own. Her long, pink tongue hung from the side of her mouth, and her chest was heaving with each breath.

She didn't bark now, but she kept watching

Whitey, as if a momentary glance away might make her lose sight of him again. Nor did she move another inch closer to the cat, as if she thought doing so might frighten him away.

Suddenly Whitey's sensitive ears picked up a new sound. As his eyes shifted away from Ginger, his pupils contracted from the brightness of the snow, his fur stood upright around his neck, and his back arched. He looked back at the dog and saw her turn too, her ears jerking, her tongue pulling back into her mouth.

A few moments later the source of the sound popped into view. Three dogs of different sizes and colors appeared from the front of the building, paused just long enough to size up the situation, then vaulted forward. Instinct alone warned the cat that the animals were after him. Their beady eyes, bared teeth, and frenzied barking as they tried to avoid Ginger and go after him, verified it.

Fear gripped him from head to tail, and his body arched more sharply, head drawn in, lips pulled back. His own white teeth were long and pointed.

"Meowrrr!" he snarled, easing back against the wall of the building.

He had been in battles before, but always with other cats. Sometimes he had fared well, sometimes not. A close examination of his back and face would reveal claw scars.

Dogs were another breed of animal. Living with the Nooleys all this time had kept him away from dogs. Ginger, who had been a pest every time they had encountered each other, was the only dog Whitey really knew.

So now encountering this trio was not only new, but terrifying. The hostile sound of their barks and the angry, fierce expressions on their faces were sure signs that they were after his hide.

The three dogs grouped together as they started forward, as if no one of them dared to take the initiative in the attack.

Whitey looked to the right of them. To the left. Escape seemed almost impossible. Yet . . .

A sudden, violent bark, unlike any the cat had ever heard before, and a fierce bolt of action startled him, freezing him momentarily to the spot. The dog, Ginger, had lunged at the middle of the three attackers, striking at his throat with open jaws and long, needle-tipped fangs.

The surprised animal slid to his side from the impact, and scrambled dizzily to regain his footing. At the same time the other two dogs switched their attention from the cat to this new, unexpected foe who until now they had probably considered too young and timid to do anything but watch. They turned upon her, biting at her side, her legs, and reaching for that vulnerable spot, her throat.

But as she fought by instinct to save the life of the cat she had wanted as a friend for a long, long time, Ginger's lightning speed and unbridled fury more than matched every snap they made. The dog she had first attacked turned and scurried away, yelping with pain. The one on the left slipped, fell, and squirmed, legs frantically clawing the air. The one on the right lunged in for an attack only to be met head on by Ginger's open jaws and strong

49

teeth that bit and drew blood. The victim yelped in pain, all four legs digging at the ground in a furious effort to break loose.

Ginger slacked her jaws and the dog escaped, bolting on the heels of its friends. Ginger chased after them, vaulting across the snow in high leaps, then stopped, and watched them run off into the adjoining field, where they eventually paused to lick their wounds.

She turned and trotted back, her tail held high in triumph. Whitey watched her, proud and grateful.

She slowed to a walk as she drew close to the cat, looking at him fondly, her tail thumping the snow-covered ground. There was a red nick on her nose, a souvenir of the battle, but it was a minor wound compared to what she must have given her enemies.

Ginger paused some three feet from Whitey, as if she still did not dare to come too close for fear he might run away. Whitey waited, then ventured forward himself. When he reached Ginger, gently, warmly, he laid his face against

51

her and rubbed against it, the soft purring inside him suggesting the strongest kind of friendship.

He heard Ginger's response, a soft whimpering sound, almost like a sob. Then Ginger licked Whitey, the ticklish sensation making the cat's back arch. He sat there, his eyes closed for a moment, thankful for this friend from another animal kingdom.

After a while he looked toward the south, instinct telling him that in that direction lay the home of the boy, his master. Without looking again at Ginger he turned and bolted down the road leading southward. He heard the dog's sudden bark and knew that she was following him, as he expected.

The wind was blowing harder now, driving the new snow, and piling it up into drifts on the gray, hard-crusted old snow.

Whitey no longer worried about his plight. Ginger was with him now.

He had no idea, though, that the two of them would not get home that night.

6

They plodded onward at the side of the road, the wind whipping their fur and showering snow against their faces. Whitey remained in the lead, with Ginger trailing protectively.

Caw! Caw!

Whitey's ears perked up, and he came to an abrupt stop. Ginger almost ran into him. Whitey looked for the source of the sound and finally saw a crow on top of a tree. He remained motionless a few seconds, ignoring Ginger's loud breathing behind him. The crow stood on its flimsy perch, its head jerking to the right, to the left. Then, as its keen eyes caught sight of the two animals, it cawed again

53

and leapt into space, wings spread wide in unhurried flight.

Disappointed, Whitey plodded on, with Ginger following. Until he had seen the crow, the cat hadn't thought about being hungry. Other things had kept him preoccupied. But the sight of the crow had brought his instincts as a predator to the surface. He wasn't home now to enjoy a delicious meal served on a platter to him by the boy. Even during those happy times, while he roamed the fields freely, a captured bird now and then satisfied a some-times unfulfilled appetite. It also proved that he hadn't lost his skill in hunting, a game he always found amusing and challenging. And, once triumphant, wholly satisfying.

The wind began to diminish in fury, but the snowflakes grew thicker, landing on the road and the fields and staying there, piling up into an ever-thickening blanket. The going got tougher. Whitey had to leap to make any prog-ress, and he stopped now and then to look behind him. Satisfied that Ginger was still with him, he would turn and go on.

A gray, hulking house loomed ahead. Usually where there was a house there was food.

Ginger must have sensed this too, for she let out a soft, joyous bark and came up alongside Whitey, her tongue hanging from her jowls. The two stood and looked at the house, their heads tilting first to one side and then to the other in silent contemplation.

Then, a decision reached, Ginger moved forward, her head held high, ears perked with alertness. Whitey watched her till she was some ten feet ahead, then meowed and leaped after her.

They walked around the house to the back where a small, dilapidated porch led to a screen door from which the screen had been partly torn. The door behind it, covered by a white curtain, was closed.

An old car was parked in the yard. Beyond it was some farm equipment that looked as if it hadn't been used in years. A barn loomed forlornly in the distance, its big door ajar.

Ginger started forward, with Whitey right behind her. Suddenly she paused, lowered her head, and sniffed at tracks in the snow. Someone had walked to the barn. Someone from the house, for the tracks were coming from the porch. But they were blurred, making it impossible to tell whether the person was still in the barn or had returned.

As if she weren't going to wait to find out, Ginger started forward again, her feet plowing thin furrows through the snow, which made Whitey's progress slightly better.

At the open door of the barn they stopped. Ginger peeked inside. Whitey came up alongside of her and peeked in, too.

They saw the animal at the same time. A German shepherd, lying on a bed of straw. Near him was an empty dish.

The dog lifted his head, pricking up his stiff, long ears. Instantly he was on his feet, barking ferociously as he bounded after the smaller dog and cat, who had had the audacity to invade his lair.

Ginger and Whitey turned and bolted away, heading for the road from where they had come. Because her longer legs provided her with the agility to leap over the snow, Ginger sprang ahead of the cat.

They hadn't gone more than sixty feet when suddenly terror seized Whitey. The German shepherd, tall, agile, and fast, was catching up with him. As the dog snapped at Whitey's head, the cat skidded to a stop and wheeled around to face the big animal, his back arched, his claws stretched out to rake.

Growling fiercely, the shepherd dove at Whitey, jaws opened wide, fangs exposed. As he lunged forward, Whitey raked him with his claws, drawing thin red furrows down the front of the shepherd's face, and the dog yelped with pain.

Whitey fell backward, squirmed to his feet, started on, and again he was attacked. The shepherd's jaws clamped about his throat now, and Whitey could feel the animal's hot breath.

Suddenly a new sound fell on the cat's ears. A familiar sound. The angry, boiling-mad cry of his friend!

The jaws relaxed from around Whitey's throat as his attacker turned to meet the young

57

squirt who had dared to attack him. The cat saw his friend hanging desperately onto the neck of the shepherd, twisting and writhing with all the power she could muster in that small young body of hers.

Believing somehow that his courageous friend would escape successfully from the shepherd, Whitey started to run toward the road. Just then the door of the house burst open and a man rushed out.

"Shep!" he yelled. "Shep! Stop that! Stop that this minute!"

Whitey paused for an instant, just long enough to turn around and see the struggle end — and Ginger bolt toward him — then turned again and ran for the road. On reaching it both animals looked back and saw the big German shepherd standing there in the yard, staring after them, tongue suspended like a wet, drooping flag. Though triumph was sure to have been his had the fight continued, he stood defeated now.

Whitey meowed softly and purred his thanks as he brushed up alongside Ginger and licked the superficial wounds on the dog's face. In return Ginger licked Whitey, and then they continued on their way, happy in their success at surviving a second ordeal which had nearly turned into a disaster.

Now, though, they were even hungrier than ever.

They plodded on, the snow falling around them as thick and soft as goosedown. Soon the wind blew less strongly than it had earlier, as if it had run its course. But each minute the snow got deeper and the going more difficult. Whitey, much shorter than Ginger, happily followed in the dog's path, but even so, he had to leap from one pair of tracks to the next. And he was tired. He wanted desperately to stop and rest, but Ginger kept going, stopping only to wait for Whitey to catch up to her, then running again as if she were anxious to close the gap between them and home before night fell.

Darkness began to set in, though, catching them unaware. Ginger proceeded more slowly now, keeping only two or three feet ahead of

Whitey, stopping frequently to look over the snow-covered terrain for a suitable spot in which to spend the night.

Now and then a whimper came from her, a soft, aching sound that Whitey interpreted as fear. The cat would go up to her and rub against her and purr, and then the whimper would stop. And Whitey, proud of his comforting instincts, would know that the ache had stopped, too.

They came to a tree at the side of the road that looked like a promising place to spend the night, but they decided it was too exposed to the elements. They rejected it and went on.

Finally they came upon a cluster of bushes under which hardly any snow had touched the ground. They crawled underneath it, examined it as much as they were able to in the darkness, found it satisfactory, and accepted it.

Ginger circled round a spot and then settled down as comfortably as she could. Whitey snuggled up beside her, curling himself into a ball. Secure and happy in each other's presence, they slept.

7

There was still some daylight left when Tommy and Jamie arrived at the Happy Place Restaurant. The snow was almost a foot deep now and getting deeper. Two cars were parked in front of the long, shallow building. A red neon sign flickered in one of the two large windows, both of which had giant snowflakes painted on them.

The boys pulled up in front. Suddenly Tommy yanked on the reins as he spotted a sign in the snow.

"Jamie, look! Tracks!"

"Could be a truck's," Jamie observed. "But there's too much snow to really tell."

Tommy looked for something to tie Buck to, saw a tree just beyond the restaurant, and rode over to it. He wrapped the reins twice around a low branch, and then he and Jamie slid off the horse.

They brushed the snow off their clothes and walked into the restaurant, the sudden warmth like a hot oven against their cold faces. A Christmas tree, glittering with lights, bulbs, and tinsels, stood in a corner of the dining room. A large red paper bell was suspended from the ceiling.

A woman stood behind the counter. She was carrying on a conversation with two men customers sitting on stools. All three turned simultaneously when the two boys entered. After a quick sizing-up of the newcomers the customers looked away and continued the conversation among themselves. The woman turned on a smile as she stepped in front of the boys. She was dark-haired, plump, and wore a white apron.

"Hi," she greeted them warmly. "Something for you boys?"

"Well, ah . . . ," Tommy faltered. What could he ask her? If she'd seen a cat come out of a truck that had stopped here? How could she have? It was miserable outdoors. Even if it hadn't been snowing she wouldn't have gone out for anything. She had to stay behind the counter.

Her smiled widened, and a look of understanding entered her blue eyes. She jerked a thumb at a machine behind her.

"Want some hot chocolate?"

"No, thanks," said Tommy.

"We're looking for a cat and a dog," Jamie said evenly. "They jumped into a truck back in Joberg, and we've been following on Tommy's horse ever since. The truck might've stopped here. Smalls?"

"Smalls? The wholesale delivery people? Yes. It stopped here. It left about half an hour ago. But I don't know about a cat or dog. I didn't see any."

Tommy's hopes withered.

"Did the man open the back of the truck?" he asked lamely. "Did he bring in anything?"

"Yes. A couple of cases of hot dogs and hamburg . . . some other meat. Why?"

"Then the animals might've left the truck."

"Or they might not have," said Jamie.

They looked at each other. How would they know?

"Wait a minute," the woman said.

She was frowning, thinking seriously. Then she looked at them, her eyes flicking from one boy to the other like a pendulum.

"I remember a lot of barking going on behind the restaurant," she said. "Like when dogs come across a cat. Then the sound changed, like a fight started. I remembered it because . . . " Her eyes widened as the memory of it came fully to her. "Oh, for heaven's sake, what's the matter with me? Of course, Mike, Smalls' delivery man, did mention that a cat and dog jumped out of his truck when he opened the door."

Tommy's heart pounded hard against the cage of his chest. "Then they *did* get out!"

"They sure did," Jamie agreed. "But which way did they go?"

Tommy grabbed his friend's arm and pulled him toward the door. "Maybe we can find their tracks, Jamie!" he cried. "C'mon!"

"Hold it, you kids," one of the men at the counter said. He wore green coveralls and had about a two-day growth of beard. "That weather out there's pretty bad, and it's getting worse every minute. You're not figgerin' on riding in that snow very long, are you?"

Tommy shrugged. "We'll ride till we find our pets," he said seriously.

"Well, it'll be dark in half an hour. Maybe less. And even a horse might have a bad time stepping through deep snow. That snow is getting deeper by the minute, kids. That's no ordinary snowfall. It's a big one. The old man of 'em all. I suggest you ride back home and forget those animals of yours. They'll make out somehow. The Man upstairs will take care of 'em. It's more important that you watch out for your own skins."

The boys looked at each other. The man was probably right, they were both thinking, but Whitey and Ginger weren't his. He didn't

66

know how strong a bond the boys felt with their animals. He didn't know the care they had taken of them ever since the animals' birth. The boys had fed, bathed, and wormed them, taken them to the vets, rescued them from enemies, done everything boys could possibly do for pets they loved very much. A parent couldn't do more for his child. How could they just "forget" those animals? They couldn't.

"Thanks, sir," Tommy said. "But we can't stop looking for 'em, now. We've got to be going. C'mon, Jamie. Let's go. And thanks, ma'am. Thanks a million."

The woman smiled. "Good luck," she said.

They ran out to the rear of the restaurant where marks in the snow, though partially covered, indicated that a struggle had taken place such as the lady in the restaurant had described. Some of the tracks led toward the woods in the direction of Danning. Another — it looked like a single track, although it was difficult to tell since fresh snow had covered it — was going almost in the opposite direction.

The opposite direction? Tommy peered as far as he could into the snow-blurred distance, darkened by the oncoming dusk. He looked back toward the road on which he and Jamie had come, then back again at the single furrow that lay in the snow. It was straight as a string, and it was leading southward — toward Joberg!

"That track, Jamie!" he yelled. "Looks like the two animals made it!"

"I see what you mean, Tommy. Could be Ginger led the way and Whitey followed."

"Right." He squinted through the gusting snow at a road that headed southward. "I think they took that road, Jamie."

"It runs parallel with the lake and goes to Overton," Jamie said. "But there are other roads that shoot down from it to the lake. If Ginger and Whitey take any of those roads they could get lost."

Overton was the city lying at the head of Lake Kelsey. It was at least twenty-five snow-blanketed, perilous miles away. The thought wrenched Tommy. The animals would never make it. Never. And if Ginger was leading — as she must be doing according to the tracks — she might take one of the roads leading down toward the lake. The dog was young and reckless sometimes. Tommy worried that she might lack the instinct that nature provided to help direct animals back to familiar territory.

Tommy bolted around to the front of the restaurant where Buck was tied. "C'mon, Jamie!" he yelled over his shoulder. "Let's go after 'em before it gets dark or we won't be able to see a thing!"

They ran to the tree, unhitched Buck, mounted him, and rode off.

"Go, Buck!" Tommy ordered, digging his heels into the horse's ribs. "Whitey's your friend, too!"

They raced over the road, the wind whistling around their ears, the snow striking their faces like pellets of powder. In a few minutes it came down thicker and harder, making it impossible to see ten feet ahead.

"Better slow 'im down, Tommy!" Jamie yelled. "Or get over to the side of the road! If a car comes toward us we'll never see it!"

Good advice, thought Tommy. *Even if a car had its headlights on, it would come upon us so quickly there might not be time enough to avoid a collision.*

He pulled gently on the right rein and Buck veered to the right. Then Tommy tugged gently on the left rein to straighten him out. Buck followed the directions obediently.

"Thataboy, Buck," Tommy said. He loved the big, friendly quarter horse as much as he loved Whitey. He would do the same for Buck if the horse were ever in this same situation, but that wasn't likely. A wood fence kept Buck safely within his bounds, and it was too high for him to jump. Nothing short of a broken fence or an open gate would ever permit the big burly animal to run loose on the countryside.

The wind and snow grew in intensity, cutting visibility down to zero. Buck slowed down on his own initiative, snapping his head up and down and whinnying in protest against further advancement. He, too, seemed to sense the danger of pursuing a road he couldn't see, and now he was too frightened to go on. He balked, reared on his hind legs, and almost dislodged Tommy from his saddle. *Good thing,* Tommy thought, *that Jamie's arms were holding me tightly or the unexpected buck would probably have thrown me off.*

"Easy, Buck!" Tommy yelled. "Easy!"

Buck didn't seem to hear, as if Tommy's voice had been drowned in the wind. He bolted again, his head and forelegs rising higher now, his whinnying cry a loud, desperate scream of fear.

Suddenly his rear legs weakened underneath him, and his scream sharpened as he started to slip to his side. Fright took hold of Tommy, and he gripped tightly to the reins. In the next instant he felt the clasped hands around his waist break loose, and heard Jamie's voice: "Jump, Tommy!"

He felt Jamie throwing himself clear of the horse. Before Tommy could follow, the horse

slipped down into a ditch, thrashing frantically in a futile effort to regain his balance.

Just as the animal fell over on his side, Tommy flung himself clear and rolled over quickly to avoid being buried by the horse or struck by his flailing legs.

He stopped when he reached the snow-covered bank on the opposite side. Now he saw that Buck, less than five feet away, was scrambling to his feet, his tail thrashing like a whip, his head snapping up and down as if trying to thrust something off it.

"Easy, Buck!" Tommy cried, trudging toward him. "Easy! I'll be right with you, boy! I'll be right with you!"

The horse calmed down a little, his large eyes seeking out Tommy as the boy got hold of his bridle.

A smile came over Tommy's snow-powdered face. "Thataboy, Buck. Just hold still a minute, you'll be all right. It's just a ditch we fell into."

He thought of Jamie, and looked over to

73

where his friend had fallen. Tommy saw a dark blur. He assumed it was Jamie, but it wasn't moving.

"Jamie!" he called, anxiety in his voice. "Hey, Jamie! You all right?"

8

The snow-distorted image moved and started to emerge from the snow.

"I'm all right, Tommy," came Jamie's voice. "How about you?"

Relief swept over Tommy. "I'm okay. Buck's pretty scared, though. I'm having a time calming him down."

Jamie trudged forward through the knee-deep snow. Tears caused by the strong wind blurred his eyes. He stepped alongside Buck and patted the animal gingerly.

"Take it easy, Buck. Everything's all right, now."

Sure, Tommy thought despairingly. *Every-*

thing's fine. We're far from anyplace, can't see a foot ahead of us, and in a few minutes it'll be dark. Nothing can be finer than that.

Even Buck couldn't be fooled about that.

In a few minutes Buck was calmed down as much as Tommy thought he could be under the circumstances. But the huge brown eyes continued to seek the boy, as if the animal needed his master's reassurance to keep him from becoming frantic again.

Tommy laid his face against Buck's. The first touch was cold, as if the fur were tipped with ice. Then he felt the warmth coming through, and he rested there a while. Tommy's eyes closed, and he felt reassured by the presence of the big, friendly animal.

"What're we going to do, Tommy?" Jamie asked.

"Keep going," Tommy said, taking his face away from Buck's. "We can't stay here. We'll freeze."

He stumbled up the side of the ditch to the road, pulling Buck by the bridle. "Come on, Buck. Up, boy."

Buck scrambled out of the ditch. Tommy sensed the tension coming back to the animal. He could see it in Buck's large, darting eyes.

"We won't ride him," Tommy decided. "We'll walk with him. He's still a little scared. Why don't you walk ahead of us, Jamie? Lead the way."

"Okay."

"Not too far ahead!"

They walked on through the blustering storm, Tommy leading Buck by the bridle. Night was still falling, blending with the bitter snowstorm.

Presently Jamie yelled above the din, "I see a light, Tommy!"

Tommy saw it, too, a blurred yellow spot in the distance. He thought at first it was a car, but it wasn't moving.

They approached the source of the light more quickly than Tommy expected. It was coming from a farmhouse set off at the left side of the road, a huge, ghostly building around which the wind sang its eerie song of winter.

They paused on the road where the wind

was less blustery, at a spot protected by a barn standing on the opposite side of the road from the house. Tommy noticed that the barn's large front door was closed.

He headed toward it, taking hold of Buck's bridle with his other hand. His left hand was numb from the cold. *Darn,* he thought, *for not bringing my gloves.*

Jamie ran ahead of him, got to the door, and tried to pull it open. It budged a little, but that was all.

Tommy noticed that it wasn't locked. Probably all it would take was more strength. He let loose of Buck and grabbed hold of the wide latch with Jamie. Together they pulled on the door. It slid open with a rasping sound.

"Far enough," Tommy said. He reached for Buck's bridle and pulled him through the narrow opening. Then he and Jamie pulled the door closed until it was within six inches of being shut.

"Let's find a place to lie down, then we'll shut it," Tommy said.

The odor of hay stung his nostrils moments before he was able to see the hundreds of bales piled up almost to the rafters. He pulled Buck after him as he and Jamie stepped across the warped, squeaking floor toward the pile. He let go of the bridle and felt around for a loose mound of hay. *I could make Buck lie down and then cover him with it,* he thought, *then Jamie and I could snuggle inside of another bundle and keep warm while we sleep through the night.*

"All the bales are tied," Jamie said from the other end of the barn.

"We'll break a couple open," Tommy said.

They got a bale and tried to pull off the cord. It was packed so tightly that they had to pull handfuls of hay out before they were able to break up the rest. In a few minutes they had the hay fixed like a huge nest.

"Okay, Buck," Tommy said, grabbing Buck's bridle and urging him to lie down. "There's your bed for the night."

Buck was slow to yield to such hospitality,

even though it was his master who was offering it to him. But eventually, apparently after reassuring himself that all this was for his own good, he lay down and made himself comfortable.

"Thataboy." Tommy patted him and covered him with the hay.

The boys broke loose another bale and nestled into it like peas in a pod. The hay protected them from the cold, and soon the heat from their bodies began to warm them up. They forgot the cold, but they remembered the cause of all this heartaching experience. Whitey and Ginger, their beloved pets.

Where were they? Could they still be walking in the storm, or had they holed up somewhere?

Where? In some other barn? Or alongside the road, under a small tree, or a bush?

They'll make out somehow, the man at the restaurant had said. *The Man upstairs will take care of 'em.*

The thought of the Man upstairs reminded

Tommy of his bedtime prayers, and he said them silently, going through them quickly because Jamie was talking.

"Sorry I didn't hear everything you said," Tommy interrupted when he finished. "I was praying."

"Well, I'll pray too, then I'll tell you what I said."

Tommy waited, wondering if their prayers were similar. Jamie's prayers were quick, that was for sure.

"I was talking about our parents, Tommy," Jamie said.

"Yeah. They're probably worried stiff about us," Tommy said. "Think we ought to phone them?"

"I think so."

"Come on."

They shoved the hay aside, feeling the nocturnal cold biting again through their clothes.

"We'll be right back, Buck," Tommy said at the dark lump on the floor and ran to the door after Jamie.

They pushed it open, stepped outside, and

pushed it shut again. As they ran across the road to the farmhouse, Tommy was suddenly aware that no lights were shining from any of the windows.

"Looks like they've gone to bed, Jamie," he said anxiously as they ascended the steps of the porch to the door. Four square pillars held up the rectangular porch roof, and above them the shingles were flapping like a thousand angry tongues.

"Looks like it," Jamie said. "Don't see any lights."

They paused in front of the wood-paneled door.

"Think we oughta wake them up?" Tommy asked.

Jamie stood with his shoulders hunched up against the wind. His lips trembled. "I would," he said.

Tommy rapped on the door.

"Knock harder," said Jamie. "If they're asleep they'll never hear that."

Tommy knocked harder. A few seconds later the door cracked open. Then it opened

wider, revealing a girl of fifteen or sixteen
years. Her eyes widened. A kerosene lamp on
a table behind her shone on her blue jeans and
checkered blouse.

"Wow!" she cried. "Come in!"

"Thanks," said Tommy.

They stepped into the house. The girl forced
the door shut against the powerful wind.

Tommy saw others in the room — a man, a

woman, and three children. The children were younger than the girl, and they were sitting around a large round table playing cards by the frail light of the kerosene lamp. The man and woman were sitting in opposite corners, the man on a leather lounge-chair with his feet propped up on a seam-torn hassock. The flame of the lamp cast dancing shadows on his angular face and on the wall behind him. The woman was in a rocking chair, a shawl around her shoulders. Her eyes looked like glowing coals as they peered out of the dark corner of the room.

In another corner stood a tall, full-branched Christmas tree hung with ornamental bulbs that glittered faintly in the light of the lamp. An array of boxes, each wrapped in the multicolors of the Christmas season and embellished with ribbons and bows, lay underneath, awaiting that moment when they would be opened and their secret contents exposed to the awestruck wonder and happy sighs of the family.

"What in blazes!" cried the man, leaning forward in his chair. "Who are you kids? What're you doing out in this kind of weather?"

Tommy said, trembling, "We — we've been looking for our animals."

The heat of the room felt so good he wished he and Jamie could stay here. They'd even sleep on the floor and not accept any food. Not even a hot chocolate drink.

"Animals?" the man echoed. "What animals?"

"My cat and Jamie's dog," Tommy answered. "They must've gone by here earlier. At least, they were headed this way."

The man slid out of his chair and stood up, the reflection of the lamp light flickering in his wide eyes. "Cat an' dog? Sure they went this way. They went up to the barn and Shep got after 'em. He would've beat 'em to a pulp if I hadn't heard 'em fightin' out there and stopped 'em."

"They okay?" Jamie inquired worriedly.

"Yes. I think so. Maybe nipped a little. Shep's a tough one." His eyes shifted from one boy to the other. "You don't mean to tell me you're lookin' for 'em in this crazy storm, do you?"

"We were," Tommy admitted, fully understanding the look in the man's eyes. He glanced at the others in the room and saw that same look. *A couple of crazy kids,* the look said. *Only crazy kids would be searching for their pets in this wild storm.*

"But we saw the barn across the road and stopped there," Tommy went on, hoping to dispel their disapproving thoughts. "We were lying in the hay awhile when Jamie said we ought to call our parents. Let them know where we are. They're probably pretty worried."

"I wouldn't be surprised," the man said. "Where do you live?"

"In Joberg."

"Joberg?" The man stared. "That's about twenty miles from here! You didn't *walk* all this way. . . . ?"

"No. We rode on Tommy's horse," Jamie said.

There was a long silence before the man said, "Oh. And where's the horse? In the barn?"

Tommy nodded, hoping it was all right. It was.

The man cleared his throat. "Well, got some sad news for you," he said. "You see that our power's off? It's been off about half an hour. A tree must have blown over and busted a wire. And if that isn't enough to curl your hair, the telephone's out, too."

9

The farmer's name was Stanley Hutchings. The daughter who had met the boys at the door was Joyce. The other children were Mary, Robert, and Stanley, Jr. They all watched in silence as Tommy and Jamie took off their galoshes and heavy coats and dropped them on the kitchen floor next to the gas range. The oven door was open and heat was pouring from it.

Mrs. Hutchings smiled from the doorway. "You boys must be pretty cold. How about some hot chocolate?"

Tommy smiled back at her. "That would taste good," he said.

"Sure would," Jamie agreed.

She cooked the hot chocolate on the range, then poured each of the boys a glassful.

"Sip it first," she advised. "It's pretty hot."

They sipped slowly, savoring the sweet chocolate taste, and enjoying its warmth as it flowed down into their empty stomachs. *I sure could dig into a hot meal now, too,* Tommy thought. He hadn't eaten since noon and didn't think that Jamie had, either.

"Have you had supper?" Mrs. Hutchings asked.

The boys looked at each other, then, together, shook their heads from side to side.

"Joyce —" Mrs. Hutchings turned to her oldest daughter "— get that casserole out of the refrigerator, and heat it up for them."

She smiled and ruffled the boys' heads, then looked at her husband. "Stan, after the boys eat, I think we'd all better get ready for bed. I'll get some blankets and put them on the floor in the dining room. Tommy and Jamie can sleep there. Maybe the electric people will fix that broken wire sometime during the night, and the furnace will pop on."

The three younger children went to bed reluctantly. Even though they hadn't had much conversation with the two visitors, they hated to part company. At last they climbed up the stairs to their rooms, each saying good night.

Joyce stayed up with her parents, collecting the dishes and glasses from the table, and carrying them to the sink when the boys were finished eating. Mrs. Hutchings got blankets and placed them on the dining room floor between the table and a wall.

"Here are enough for you to lie on and to cover yourselves with," she said, fixing them for the boys. "Keep your pants and shirts on if you like, but you'd better take off your shoes."

They said good night and retired, Joyce upstairs, and Mr. and Mrs. Hutchings into a room adjoining the living room. The boys took off their shoes and crawled between the covers. The kerosene lamp was still lit.

"They're sure nice," Jamie said softly.

"Sure are," Tommy agreed.

Silence awhile.

"This floor's hard as a rock," Tommy whispered.

"Maybe you'd rather sleep out there in the barn," Jamie said.

"At least the straw is soft," Tommy replied.

He closed his eyes and thought of his mother and father. They were probably worrying their heads off about him. Jamie's parents must be worrying, too. By now both families had probably telephoned each other, wondering if one or the other had heard anything from the boys. They might have even notified the police by now.

"Maybe we shouldn't have done what we did, Jamie," Tommy whispered.

"Why don't you fall asleep?"

"I can't."

"Neither can I. I keep thinking about our pets."

"I was thinking about our parents," Tommy said.

"Them, too," Jamie replied. "They're probably going crazy worrying about us."

"Ever been away from home before, Jamie?"

"A few times. But my mom an' dad always knew where I was."

"Where did you go?"

"To my grandma's. Used to go there a lot when we lived in Endicott. What about you?"

"A few times, too. But never for long. Two or three days was the longest."

They were quiet awhile.

"What does your father do, Jamie?" Tommy asked at last.

"He works with the phone company. What does your father do?"

"Works with the gas company." Tommy paused. "You got something special in mind you'd like for Christmas, Jamie?"

"Yeah, I sure do."

Tommy stared at a dancing shadow on the ceiling.

"What?" he asked.

"That we find Ginger and Whitey. I don't

care if I don't get anything else, I hope we find
them safe and sound."

"Me, too," Tommy said.

"Tommy, suppose, though — just suppose
we don't find them," said Jamie. "What will
we do?"

"You can't think that way," Tommy said.
"That's thinking negative. You've got to think
positive. You've got to *believe* that we'll find
'em."

"You really believe we will?"

Tommy swallowed. That was the only thing
he could believe. He couldn't make himself
believe that their animals were dead, could he?

His throat ached, and his eyes got blurry.
"Yeah," he whispered, not really knowing
what to think. "I — I really believe we will."

Silence again, while Tommy's mind roamed
back to his parents. Mr. Hutchings had said
that his farm was about twenty miles from
Joberg. But could distance be measured in
miles for Tommy's and Jamie's parents who
didn't know where the boys were?

"I hope they find that broken wire and get

95

it fixed," Jamie said. "This floor is getting colder by the minute."

Sometime later they fell asleep.

The house was warm when they got up. It was daylight, and the wind was blowing outside. There were sounds coming from the kitchen, and there was a smell of hot coffee and cooked food. The boys peeked over their covers into the next room and saw that Mr. and Mrs. Hutchings were already up, having breakfast.

They crawled out of the blankets, put on their shoes, and went into the kitchen. The Hutchings greeted them with a jolly good morning and expressed surprise that they were up so early.

"What time is it?" Tommy asked.

"Seven-thirty," Mr. Hutchings said. His whiskered face wrinkled in a smile. "Feel better this morning? The furnace turned on about four-thirty."

Tommy grinned. "A lot warmer, anyhow!"

"Want to call your folks and tell 'em you're

96

okay?" Mrs. Hutchings asked. "The phone's working, too."

Tommy's face brightened. "Yes, thanks."

She pointed to the wall phone just inside the dining room door. He went to it and dialed the number which he knew by heart.

"Hi, Mom, this is Tommy," he said when his mother answered.

"Tommy! Oh, son!"

He heard nothing for a moment then, except what sounded like a sob.

"Mom? You okay?"

"Yes," she said, and sniffled. "I'm okay. We — we've been worried about you and Jamie, Tommy. Where are you?"

"At the Hutchings farm."

"On Phelps Road," Mr. Hutchings whispered.

"On Phelps Road," echoed Tommy.

"Dear God! Way over there?"

"We're okay, Mom. We slept here last night."

"And Buck?"

"He's out in the barn. We'll be leaving right after breakfast."

"Did you find the animals?"

"No."

"Do you want Dad to come after you?"

"No. We'll ride home on Buck. Don't worry. We'll make it all right."

"Are you sure?"

"Yes, I'm sure. I'll hang up now, Mom. Tell Jamie's mother we're okay."

"I'll call her right away," his mother promised. "Hurry home, Tommy."

" 'Bye, Mom."

"Now, sit down," said Mrs. Hutchings as he hung up, "and I'll get you boys some breakfast."

She fried eggs and toasted bread. A small radio on the counter was on, and an announcer was giving the regional news. After he spoke about the town council and some new laws legislated by them, he started reporting about "the two boys who had disappeared during the night and were still not heard from."

Tommy and Jamie paused as their names were announced. They heard that they were the subjects of an intensive search being conducted throughout the whole county. "They were on Tommy's horse," the announcer explained, "and may have stayed overnight in the woods somewhere. Anyone seeing the two boys and the horse please notify the sheriff's department immediately."

"Well, you made the news," Mr. Hutchings said, smiling. "And you'll make it again when they find out that you've been located." He chuckled dryly.

After breakfast the boys put on their coats and galoshes, thanked Mrs. Hutchings for her warm hospitality, and went out with Mr. Hutchings to the barn. Mr. Hutchings took a pail of water with him. The wind had died down some, and there was evidence that a snowplow had passed through on the road sometime during the night. Tommy fervently wished that it would pass through again soon.

They found Buck eating the hay, and Mr. Hutchings laughed. "Say! Mighty fine looking horse you've got there! And he ain't dumb, either! Believes in helping himself!"

Tommy smiled and patted Buck affectionately as Mr. Hutchings placed the pail of water on the floor. "Go to it, boy," Mr. Hutchings said, and Buck did.

Tommy was anxious to leave and continue the search for Whitey and Ginger. When Buck was finished, Tommy and Jamie thanked the farmer for putting them up for the night, and then they both got on Buck and rode out of the barn.

Mrs. Hutchings and the children were looking through the window, waving. The boys waved back, then started their trek on the snow-drifted road toward Overton. About two-thirds of the way there they would swing left to Joberg. And home. They would either find Whitey and Ginger on the way, or they wouldn't.

We don't know where else to look, Tommy thought, his heart aching. *There's nothing else to do but go home and maybe continue the search later.*

10

Whitey and Ginger slept through the night, little disturbed by the howling wind. Only Ginger's whimpering, caused by her dreams, stirred Whitey to wakefulness a few times during the night. Other than that, both slept peacefully.

It was dawn when the earth trembled beneath them, and a thunderous roar brought them both awake. Wide-eyed and frightened, Whitey stood up and saw that their temporary home was completely covered with snow except for a small opening on one side, the side opposite the one from which the wind was blowing. The opening was barely large enough for Whitey to poke his face through, but it widened easily as he forced himself through it.

The louder the sound grew the more the earth trembled. Looking about him Whitey saw a blinking yellow light on top of a gigantic yellow monster. It crept up the road toward them, thrusting the snow to the side in one continuous, spiraling twist.

Fearing that the monster might be after them, Whitey meowed a warning to Ginger, leaped out of the snow-covered quarters, and dashed into the woods. Ginger barked, acknowledging the warning. They ran on and on, Whitey leading the way, until he realized that the thunderous roar was growing more distant, and the tremble of the earth had ceased.

Whitey paused beside a bush and looked back at the dog who came up beside him, eyes bright and shiny, tongue suspended from the side of her jaw, tail wagging. They looked at each other, pleased in their own way with each other's presence and happy that they were safe from the monster that had awakened them and chased them out of their nest.

Suddenly a new sound attracted their attention and made their ears perk. Together they looked in the direction of the sound, and both saw its source at the same time.

It was a bird. A fair-sized one. If captured it could provide a decent meal. There wouldn't be enough to satisfy both cat and dog, but a little for each was better than nothing.

Whitey crouched down on his haunches, so low and so white that he blended in well with the snow environment. He waited a few moments, watching the bird peck at the snow-covered ground, lift its head, look sharply around, then peck again. This behavior on the part of bird was most annoying. That peck and look were cautionary measures that kept it safe from harm.

Whitey watched, his thoughts on the meal that a delicious morsel of bird would provide. When the bird lowered its beak to peck at the ground again, the cat moved stealthily forward, his belly so low it scraped the snow. When the bird lifted its head, the cat stopped.

This silent, stealthy maneuver continued until the cat was within twenty feet of the bird. Then the bird, upon raising its head for the umpteenth time, stood frozen. Its right eye had seen the cat. And, although the cat stood as motionless as a statue, the bird seemed to sense that the white, furry animal wasn't there by accident.

Without another second's delay, the bird chirped and flew off. Whitey, disappointed, watched it fly onto a high branch where it shrilled a few notes of mockery and flew off again.

Whitey returned to Ginger's side, and saw that Ginger hadn't moved from the spot where he had left her.

They stood there, the wind howling around them, lifting their fur, sending sprays of snow up around their legs. Now that the sight of the bird had whetted his appetite, Whitey's hunger pangs grew. But there was another feeling that bothered him, too. His longing for his master was even stronger than his hunger.

He looked about him but saw nothing but trees and brush and drifted snow. The place was totally strange and far, far away from home.

"*Meow!*" he cried softly, ruefully.

He looked at Ginger and saw in her big, sad-looking eyes friendliness and compassion. He appreciated her companionship and was grateful for the times she had fought against powerful odds to save both herself and him from those ruthless dogs.

But now they had to move on. They had to return to the road, for something told him it was that road that would eventually lead them home.

They retraced their steps back to the bush where they had slept last night, then paused at the side of the ditch nearby, now covered by a high mound of snow. The monster did that, thought Whitey — it had created a mountain of snow that blocked passage to the road.

With Ginger beside him he studied the high white fortress in front of him, then sprang forward, scrambling up to its peak, where he paused briefly and looked at the road that was now cleared of snow. The wind whipped white powder into his face and ruffled his fur. He glanced up and down the road, saw nothing but the drifting snow, and slid down the slope to the road, creating a miniature avalanche in his wake. Ginger followed him. At the bottom they paused to get their bearings, then headed south on a trot.

Tommy and Jamie braced themselves against the wind, riding on the road which the snowplow had cleared only moments ago. They rode silently, each thinking thoughts about his own pet, and neither one believing he'd ever see his pet again. Their hearts ached with grief.

Some one hundred yards ahead was the yellow snowplow, thrusting the snow into the ditch at the left-hand side of the road. Wisps of snow swirled angrily in its wake, building up slowly into drifts.

Buck plodded on, his hoofs striking the plowed road with a muffled, rhythmic sound.

"Think we'll ever see them again, Tommy?" Jamie asked.

"We can't think any other way, Jamie," Tommy answered. "We'll have to think that we'll see them again."

"And if we don't?"

"We don't, that's all."

They rode on a few more minutes before Jamie spoke again. "Tonight's Christmas Eve. It'll be the saddest Christmas I've ever had."

"Me, too."

"Yes, but you've still got Buck," Jamie said. "He'll help you forget that cat."

"He wasn't just 'that cat,'" Tommy retorted. "He was smart. Sometimes he looked at me like he wanted to talk. And lots of times I knew just what he was thinking. We were close, Whitey and me. We were pals. What am I saying? We *are* pals! I'm talking as if he's dead and gone!"

"Ginger and I are pals, too," Jamie said. "Only thing is, she's still young. She wants to play all the time. I've been teaching her to fetch and to shake hands."

A lump rose in Tommy's throat. "It was her fault that Whitey ran into that truck," he said, not realizing he was saying it till he heard the words. "She would never have . . ."

"Are you blaming Ginger?" Jamie interrupted, his voice raised a little. "Are you blaming her for your cat hopping up into that truck?"

"Well, whose fault was it if it wasn't hers?" Tommy snapped. "If Ginger didn't aggravate Whitey he would've stayed right in that same spot until I came out of the store."

"Aggravate Whitey?" Jamie echoed. "That's a hot one! That young pup couldn't aggravate anybody! She was just being friendly, I tell you! She wanted to play! I know she did!"

"Play or not, she . . . " Tommy cut the sentence short, realizing that this argument between him and Jamie was getting all out of proportion. He had better stop now before it led to something both would regret for a long time.

"Jamie."

"I think you'd better stop Buck," said Jamie. "I'll walk the rest of the way home. It isn't . . . "

"Jamie! Listen! Let's not say anymore about it!" Tommy yelled. "We haven't argued all this time! We'd better not start now!"

Jamie was silent a minute. "I guess you're right," he said at last, his voice barely audible above the wind. "And this is no place to argue. I really wouldn't want to walk home from here, anyway."

Tommy heard his laughter mix with the sound of the wind, and he grinned. "Don't worry about that," he said, much relieved.

Up ahead a road branched off to the left of the one they were on. The snowplow had driven on it a little and was now backing up and returning in their direction.

"There's the road to Joberg," Tommy said.

"And home," Jamie added.

Tommy reined Buck to the right side of the road, then pulled the horse to a dead stop as he saw that Buck was disturbed by the oncoming snowplow. The boys exchanged waves with the two men in the truck as it went by, then they rode on, turning to the left at the junction where a sign on a thin metal pole read, *Joberg*.

"Wouldn't it be wonderful if we found our pets home waiting for us?" Jamie said.

The thought lifted Tommy's hopes, although he was certain that that was too much to expect.

"It would be, Jamie," he admitted. "But they're not home. They couldn't have walked all the way home from that restaurant in that blizzard last night, and they weren't on the road this morning because we didn't see them." He swallowed a lump that had risen in his throat. "Like you said, Jamie . . . it's going to be a sad Christmas. A real sad Christmas."

They pulled into Joberg some fifteen minutes later, and five minutes after that they rode by Tommy's house on their way to Jamie's.

They looked to see if anyone was watching from the windows, and elation filled Tommy's heart as he saw his mother and father, smiling and waving at them.

"Hi, Mom! Hi, Dad!" he shouted against the strong wind.

They rode up the road to Jamie's house and into the snow-drifted driveway, where Jamie slid off the horse.

"Thanks, Tommy!" he yelled and ran to the house, where his mother was already at the door, her face wreathed with a joyous smile as she held it open for him.

Tommy rode back to his house, put Buck in the barn, and ran to the front door, where his mother and father greeted him like a long-lost son.

"Whitey isn't here, is he, Mom?" he asked breathlessly. "We were hoping . . . "

"No, he isn't," said his mother, her blue eyes blurred with happy tears. "But you are."

"We've called the radio station in Overton, though," said his father. "There's a notice out for him and Jamie's dog on the radio. If anybody sees them he's to notify us right away."

There was a lump in Tommy's throat. He blinked, pulled himself away from his parents, and walked into the living room where a short, stubby Christmas tree filled a corner of the room. Beneath it boxes of various sizes were piled up, each wrapped in colorful wrapping paper and tied with satiny ribbons.

He choked back tears. Nothing in those boxes would make up for the loss of Whitey. Nothing.

"Come. Let's take off your galoshes and coat," his mother said.

He went to the kitchen and took them off. "Mom," he said, "have you ever visited Mrs. Gilman, Jamie's mother?"

Her eyes met his and held them. "A little."

"If she's anything like — Jamie — or if his father's anything like him — they must be okay."

She smiled. "Nobody said they weren't. What made you bring that up?"

113

He thought of his and Jamie's adventure which had begun before nightfall yesterday and ended just a little while ago.

"It's the first time I've ever spent so much time with Jamie. He's a real nice kid."

"Maybe we'll get together sometime," his mother said. "Have a picnic or something."

"I think he'd like that," Tommy said.

Suddenly he listened. He could hear the wind, but wasn't there another sound with it?

He heard it again. A *bark!*

He ran to the front door, yanked it open, and rushed out to the porch. And there, running up the road, came the two animals — Whitey and Ginger!

"Mom, Dad, they're here!" Tommy shouted, his eyes blurring. "Whitey and Ginger are home!"

He stood on the porch waiting for them, and Whitey rushed up and leaped into his arms, purring as he had never purred before.

"Oh, Whitey!" Tommy cried happily, hugging him. "Am I glad to see you!"

He saw Ginger standing in the road, tongue hanging out, tail wagging, eyes shiny with eagerness.

"Hurry home, Ginger!" Tommy yelled. "There's somebody waiting for you, too!"

He laughed as the dog sprinted off toward the house a short distance up the road, ears pressed back against her head as if she were running the race of her life.

Tommy saw Jamie stepping out onto the porch, and Ginger rushing up to meet him, jumping up and licking her master. She was so jubilant and thrilled it certainly must have been the most happy moment of her life. And Jamie's, too.

Jamie looked up and waved, and Tommy waved back. Then Tommy hugged his cat and carried him into the house.

Mom and Dad looked at him, both trying hard to control their emotions.

"It's really a Merry Christmas, after all, Tommy," Mom said.

"Yes, Mom. It really is."